This is a book about different types of cake. If you like to **EAT** cake or **BAKE** cake then this is the book for you.

Warning—this book may make you **HUNGRY** . . .

OXFORD
UNIVERSITY PRESS

Great Clarendon Street, Oxford OX2 6DP

Oxford University Press is a department of the University of Oxford.
It furthers the University's objective of excellence in research, scholarship,
and education by publishing worldwide. Oxford is a registered trade mark of
Oxford University Press in the UK and in certain other countries

Copyright © Harriet Whitehorn and Oxford University Press 2020
Illustrations © Alex G Griffiths 2020

The moral rights of the author have been asserted

First published 2020

Database right Oxford University Press (maker)

British Library Cataloguing in Publication Data
Data available

ISBN: 978-0-19-277203-9

1 3 5 7 9 10 8 6 4 2

Printed by CPI Group (UK) Ltd, Croydon CR0 4YY

Paper used in the production of this book is a
natural, recyclable product made from wood
grown in sustainable forests.
The manufacturing process conforms to the
environmental regulations of the country of origin.

FREDDIE'S AMAZING BAKERY

DANCING WITH DOUGHNUTS

WRITTEN BY
HARRIET WHITEHORN

OXFORD
UNIVERSITY PRESS

ILLUSTRATED BY
ALEX G GRIFFITHS

Our story is set in a town called *Belville* — look, here is a map of it. As you can see, it is a delightful place, just the right size, and criss-crossed by a spider's web of pretty canals (perfect for boating in summer and skating in winter), which are lined with cherry trees and tall old houses.

MAGNOLIA CANAL

BELVILLE THEATRE

BELVILLE MUSEUM

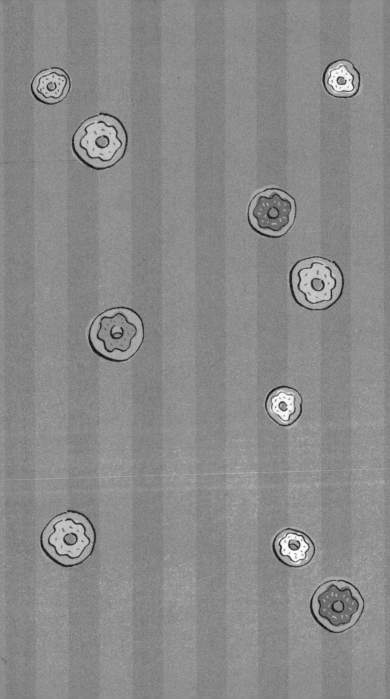

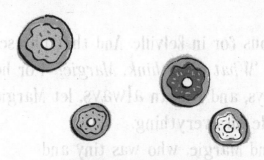

CHAPTER ONE

It was July in Belville, which meant blue skies and sunshine, long lazy days in the park, boating on the canals, and, perhaps best of all, the Summer Talent Show!

The show was run by Max Motion and his wife Margie, the owners of Belville's theatre. Max was small with a great whoosh of black hair streaked with white like a badger, and piercing blue eyes. He was a man of few words, except for one phrase that he was famous for in Belville. And that phrase was, *'What d'ya think, Margie?'* For he always, and I mean always, let Margie decide on everything.

And Margie, who was tiny and formidable, with immaculate grey hair and a pout of red lipstick, would always tell Max in no uncertain terms exactly what she thought about everything.

Everyone **loved** Max and Margie because they were great fun and did so much for Belville—they were constantly organizing not only all the normal plays, ballets, and musicals that you would expect, but also charity performances and fundraising events. Margie had a particular passion for dancing, and she often said that she wanted to get the whole of Belville dancing. So, when the couple announced that they would be retiring after the Summer Show to go on the round-the-world cruise that they'd always dreamt of, everyone was a little sad but determined to make sure that it was the best show **ever**.

Now, I should tell you that the Belville Summer Talent Show wasn't a typical talent show—there were no winners or losers—it was just a chance for anyone who lived in the town to show off their skills. It took place on the last Saturday in July, and the auditions for the acts were held ten days before. And this is where our story begins, across town at Freddie's Amazing Bakery, half an hour before the auditions were due to start . . .

It was evening, and Freddie (our hero and very talented boy baker) and his assistant Sophie were closing up the bakery after a busy day. Flapjack, Freddie's dog, was following them around, helpfully 'sweeping' up any food that had fallen on the floor.

Closing up was one of Freddie's favourite times of day at the bakery. He found it satisfying folding the tables and chairs outside the shop and stacking them in a neat pile, cleaning up the counters, and then going into the kitchen and checking everything was spotless, ready for the morning. Sophie did a quick stock check while Freddie took a batch of cinnamon buns that he had baked for everyone auditioning for the show out of the oven. He was just packing them into a cardboard box when a voice said, 'How do I look?'

Freddie turned around to see his friend and bakery manager, Amira, dressed in black trousers and tailcoat with a white waistcoat and white shirt, a bow tie, and sparkly high-heeled shoes. She was holding a walking cane and a shiny black top hat.

'You look fantastic!' Freddie said, because she did.

'Really? I'm worried that I should wear a dress,' Amira said.

'Absolutely not,' Sophie reassured her. 'The suit looks much cooler. Samuel is going to love it.'

Samuel was great friends with Amira, Sophie, and Freddie and he ran the local bookshop, as well as being Amira's dance partner.

'How are you feeling? Nervous?' Freddie asked.

'A little bit, but excited too,' replied Amira. 'Ever since I was a little girl, it's been my dream to dance in the Summer Talent Show. The auditions this evening are my chance to make that dream come true!'

'I'm sure it will—you two have worked so hard,' said Freddie.

'So, Freddie, do you wish you'd trained Flapjack to do some tricks?' Sophie asked. 'You two would make a brilliant double act.'

Freddie sighed. 'I would love to be able to do that, but I get such **terrible** stage fright that even the thought of going on stage makes me feel sick. I know I should try and get over it, but it never seems the right time to take the plunge.'

'But you managed at the baking competition,' Amira pointed out.

'I know, but baking is different,' he said with a smile. 'I never really get that nervous baking. And also, there were lots of other people on the stage, so the audience wasn't looking at just me.'

Freddie glanced up at the kitchen

clock. 'We should get going, shouldn't we? You don't want to be late for Samuel.' He picked up the box of buns.

'You're right,' Amira said. 'Thanks for closing up the shop, Sophie. You're a star.'

'No problem,' Sophie replied. 'Good luck!'

'Thank you!' Amira said. And after saying goodbye, Freddie, Flapjack, and Amira went on their way.

It was a warm summer evening, and the streets were thronging with people taking evening strolls, chatting with friends, and eating ice cream. Freddie and Amira passed lots of people they knew, who called out 'Good luck!' to Amira.

Belville's Theatre was all lit up like a Christmas tree, and the billboard on the outside read, in large letters, 'Summer Talent Show Auditions'.

There was one large dressing room backstage, and all the performers were gathered there. Freddie looked around at the familiar faces—there was Mr Poots the optician, who had transformed into a fire-eating juggler in a flame-coloured bodysuit; and the Khan sisters, who worked in the fish and chip shop, warming up for their gymnastics act. Clarabelle Cooper, the florist, was singing operatic scales in the corner, and Mr Evans, who ran the garage, was dressed in the black-and-white clothes and make-up of a mime artist.

Samuel was already there and came straight over to them. He was wearing the same outfit as Amira, minus the sparkly shoes.

'You look great,' Amira said to him.

'Thanks. So do you!' he replied. 'Shall

we just have a quick practice? We are on
in about ten minutes.'

Freddie decided it was a good moment
to hand around the cinnamon buns.

'How delicious!'

'Yummy!'

Someone even joked, 'This is definitely
your talent, Freddie!' and everyone
laughed.

There was one bun left, and Freddie
went to see if there was anyone waiting
in the wings who wanted it. But when
he got there, he saw a familiar figure
watching the dance group on the stage.
Bernard. Freddie was about to slip away,
but Bernard saw him and said, 'Freddie!
What are you doing sneaking around?'

'Hi, Bernard,' Freddie replied, and as he didn't want to be rude he went over to join him by the stage.

'Gosh, what a fantastic group of dancers!' Freddie exclaimed.

'Really?' Bernard replied. 'I was just thinking how bad they were. In fact, I can't believe how terrible the acts are this year.'

Freddie decided not to reply to this and said instead, 'Would you like this last cinnamon bun?'

'Certainly not,' Bernard replied, curling his lip with distaste, although he could feel his mouth watering. 'You know I can't bear your baking.'

You've probably got a taste of Bernard's personality by now, but you should also know that he was a baker too—

unfortunately not a very good one—his patisserie, Macaroon's, was usually empty, except for a few tourists wondering why they were eating such expensive, tasteless cakes. As a result, he was super competitive with Freddie.

Freddie was about to excuse himself and find someone nicer to talk to when he noticed that Bernard was dressed in a black suit with a tailcoat, just like Amira and Samuel.

'Are you dancing?' Freddie asked him.

'No, although I did consider it as I am a very talented dancer. I'm doing a completely brilliant magic act instead. Otto is assisting me.'

Otto was Bernard's cat. He was sitting on a box of props looking very grumpy, despite

the jaunty silver bow tie that Bernard
had put on him. He hissed extravagantly
at Flapjack and puffed his fur out like a
pom-pom. Flapjack ignored him.

'I didn't know you liked magic,'
Freddie said to Bernard.

'It's my new passion,' Bernard said.
'Of course, I'm pretty fantastic at it,
and I thought I'd try and bring a bit of
real talent to the Summer Show.'

Freddie smiled a little to himself
and replied, 'I can't wait to see your
act.'

'Yes,' Bernard continued. 'It wouldn't
surprise me if the Motions offered me
my very own show. Anyway, what's your
act? Are you and that mutt of yours
doing something together?'

He looked at Flapjack scornfully.

'Oh no, I'm not auditioning,'
Freddie replied. 'I would love to but
I get such terrible stage fright that I
can't.'

'Do you really?' Bernard said,

a triumphant smile on his face. 'Poor you!' he sniggered. 'So what are you doing here then?'

'Oh, I'm supporting Amira. She's doing a dance routine with Samuel,' he replied.

Bernard had a whopping crush on Amira, and his whole face lit up like a light bulb.

'Is she here?' he asked excitedly, craning his neck to see over Freddie's head.

Then he gasped slightly. 'Here she comes!' He started to smooth down his hair.

'Good evening, Amira,' he gushed. 'You look fantastic.'

'And so do you, Bernard,' Amira replied politely. 'That's a lovely suit you're wearing.'

'Isn't it?' he replied smugly. 'Tippy Top Tailors made it for me.'

Meanwhile, on stage, the previous act had finished.

'*What d'ya think, Margie?*' they heard Max Motion say. There was a pause, and the dancers all held their breath.

'Fantastic, guys! How would you like to open the show?'

Bernard spluttered. 'What? Honestly I think the Motions are losing their touch—it's a good thing they're retiring.'

Before anyone else could say anything, a stagehand appeared. 'Right, Bernard, you're on now,' she said. Bernard picked up Otto and his box of tricks, and marched on to the stage.

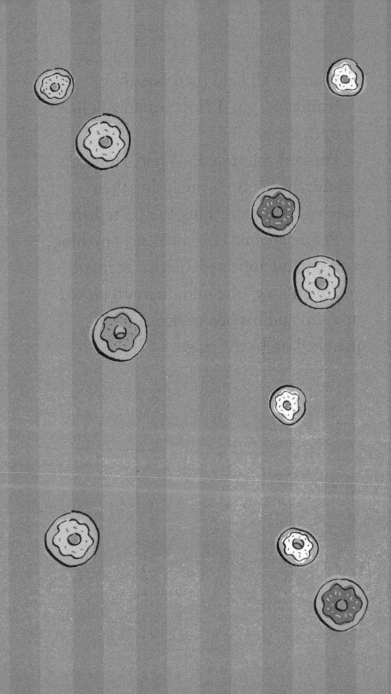

CHAPTER TWO

'Please could you read this out? It's my introduction,' Bernard said to the stagehand as he gave her a piece of paper.

'Er . . . sure,' the stagehand replied and began to read.

'Ladies and gentlemen! Prepare to be astounded and amazed, to have your mind bent and your senses turned upside down by the one and only, the stupendous Bernard the Brilliant, and his assistant Otto!'

'Wow! I'm excited!' Margie said, and

Max clapped politely.

'Thank you, thank you, you are too kind,' Bernard said pompously. 'I am Bernard the Brilliant, and may I introduce you to my handsome assistant, Otto.'

Now, no one apart from Bernard would describe Otto as handsome. He had a funny, grumpy, squished-up face and a large, rather shapeless body, a bit like an old cushion. So when Bernard said this, Margie and Max laughed loudly, thinking he was joking. A look of intense irritation passed across Bernard's face, but he tried to cover it with a smile and pressed on.

'I will begin with a card trick. Could I ask for a volunteer, please?' he said to the Motions.

'Ooh, me please,' Margie replied, springing up from her chair and walking on stage.

'Excellent, thank you, madam,' Bernard replied, pulling out a pack of cards. He began to shuffle them in a fancy way, but unfortunately he dropped them all on the ground. Margie laughed. Bernard went a little red in the face as he struggled to pick up the cards. Once he had them all, he put them into a fan shape that he thrust in front of Margie. 'Pick a card, any card.' Margie pointed to one. 'Now take it out, look at it, don't show me, and then put it back,' Bernard instructed. Margie did as she was told. Bernard shuffled the pack, did some abracadabra-ing, and then cut the pack in two, revealing the queen of hearts.

'Ta-da!' he said.

'I'm sorry, that's not my card,' Margie replied, with a jokey shake of her head.

'Are you sure?' Bernard asked, frowning.

'Quite positive,' Margie replied.

'How extraordinary!' Bernard said, in a tone of voice that implied that she must have got it wrong. 'Very well, I will cut the pack again,' he said with a slight sigh. Bernard did some finger-waggling and held up the ten of spades.

Margie giggled and shook her head. 'Nope, it's not that one either.'

Bernard's face twitched with irritation, but he knew better than to be rude to

Margie, so he said jokily, 'Just testing, dear lady.'

He cut the cards yet again, trying not to look flustered, and then said with all the determination he could muster:

'I think you'll find this is it—the two of diamonds!' he added with a flourish.

'Sorry, hon, it was the four of clubs,' Margie replied.

'Of course, I knew that,' Bernard replied crossly, and then he took a deep breath, trying to control his anger.

Then he said in as jolly a voice as he could, 'Time for another trick, I think.'

'Do you need me for this?' Margie asked.

'No thank you, dear lady,' he replied, and Margie walked back to her seat. 'For my next trick, I shall make my assistant Otto disappear. Otto, let us get you into this cage,' Bernard announced, producing a large, old-fashioned birdcage from his prop box, and placing it on top.

Otto gave Bernard a look as if to say, *There's no way I'm getting into that,* and before Bernard could grab him, the cat jumped down and made a dash for the wings. The Motions burst into laughter.

'There goes the disappearing cat!' Margie joked.

Luckily, Freddie caught Otto. He handed him, hissing and spitting, back to Bernard, who was looking rather frazzled. Bernard took the cat back to the cage and tried to stuff him into it.

But Otto wasn't going in quietly. He growled and went as rigid as a statue. The Motions thought it was hilarious, as Bernard, red-faced and sweating, attempted to shove Otto in. It was a close thing, but Bernard eventually won and shut the cage door. He then covered the cage with a large silk scarf that meant that Otto couldn't be seen, but he could still very much be heard, making his angry cat noises.

Bernard wiped his sweaty brow with a handkerchief and pulled out a wand from his pocket. Putting on his best dramatic voice, he said, 'ABRACADABRA!' and sharply tapped the cage.

Bernard was so flustered that he didn't realize that he'd pulled the trick wand he'd been saving for the finale out of his pocket. It suddenly exploded, and he jumped out of his skin and made a little yelping noise, as the wand showered him in confetti.

Max and Margie roared with laughter again, and Margie whispered to Max,

'Is this guy for real? How can he keep a straight face?'

Bernard irritably dusted the confetti off his coat and repeated 'ABRACADABRA!' as he tapped his wand on the cage again. Bernard wasn't sure whether he'd accidentally hit the wrong bit of the cage, or if Otto had got lucky and stood on a button, but either way, the sides of the cage fell down dramatically with a loud clank, and the silk scarf dropped, covering Otto. Sensing his chance to escape the stage, Otto bounded off the prop box and darted in the other direction this time so Freddie couldn't catch him, the silk scarf trailing behind him. Margie and Max hooted with laughter as Bernard dived after his beloved Otto.

'What d'ya think, Margie?' Max

Motion said.

'Hilarious! He's a comic genius, and I just love that ugly cat. It's got such a funny, squished-up, grumpy face. Let's give him a five-minute slot between the talking parrot and the kung fu fighters.'

'OK,' Max replied. 'We seem to have lost the magician—can someone please clear his stuff off the stage? Thank you!'

Freddie was sure that Bernard would be happy to hear that he'd be performing in the show, even if the act hadn't gone quite as he'd hoped. He was thinking of going to look for him when he heard Max shout:

'Right, next act please— Samuel and Amira!'

'That's us!' Samuel said nervously. 'Ready, Amira?' Amira nodded, and Freddie wished them good luck as they strolled on to the stage, swinging their canes. They took off their top hats, bowed, and introduced themselves. The music started . . .

There may be trouble ahead,
But while there's music and moonlight
And love and romance,
Let's face the music and dance . . .

They began their routine. Their dance was rather clever: it started off as an old-fashioned routine, like you'd see in a black-and-white film, but then about halfway through the music changed and the pair threw their hats and canes to one side and began a modern dance routine.

That's just fantastic! Freddie thought as he watched them. He glanced over at Max and Margie, whose eyes were glued to Amira and Samuel, mesmerized. He could also see Bernard holding Otto on the opposite side of the stage, Bernard's eyes shiny with emotion at seeing Amira dance so beautifully.

The routine finished with a **spectacular** lift where Samuel held Amira above his head—it was very difficult for both of them, and Freddie knew they had been worried about it, but they managed it beautifully. Everyone who was watching—Max and Margie, Freddie, and all the stagehands—cheered and applauded loudly when they finished.

'What d'ya think, Margie?' Max asked with a smile when the clapping died down.

'What do I think? I think you guys are **amazing**!' Margie exclaimed. 'You are by far the best act we've seen, and I think you should close the show!'

Amira gasped with delight and cried, 'Thank you so much!' while Samuel grinned from ear to ear. They began to

walk off the stage when—oh dear—
something happened . . . or to be more
precise, Otto happened.

Everyone else may have loved
watching Amira and Samuel dance, but
Otto hadn't. He was hot and bothered
and bored, and Bernard was holding
him too tightly. And he could also see
his old enemy Flapjack across the other
side of the stage, and he wanted to go
and be rude to him. So in a moment
of frustration, he did something very
wicked. He bit Bernard. Hard.

'Owww!' yelped Bernard, as Otto's
sharp little teeth sank into his finger. He
dropped the cat, who then dashed on to
the stage.

Amira and Samuel were so distracted
by the wonderful thought of closing the
show that they didn't see Otto diving

across their path, and they both tripped over him. Amira managed to avoid falling, but Samuel tumbled backwards, twisting his ankle.

'OWWWW,' he cried.

Everyone gasped. 'Was that the ugly cat? Magician man, you need to have it on a lead!' Margie exclaimed.

'Poor Otto!' Bernard cried, rushing over to the cat, who was hissing furiously at Samuel. Bernard scooped him up. 'Are you OK, my poor little man? Did that mean dog Flapjack scare you?'

Amira looked at Bernard as if he were mad. 'Samuel, are YOU OK?' she asked.

'Yes,' he replied with a sigh. 'But my ankle's not.'

The stagehand came over and examined it.

'I think it's sprained, I'm afraid.'

'Oh no!' Amira said, and Samuel looked downcast.

'You need to ice it immediately, and you should be fine,' Margie said.

'Come on, Samuel, let's get you home,' Amira said, and Freddie rushed over to help her get Samuel to his feet and off the stage. Bernard bent down to pick up Otto.

'That's such a shame for Samuel—he's a really talented dancer. I hope that he's going to be OK,' said Margie to Max.

'Sprained ankles can be really tricky,' Max replied with a grimace. 'Sadly I rather think that Amira is going to be looking for a new partner.'

A slow grin spread across Bernard's face as he strolled off stage.

'What a good boy you are!' he said to Otto.

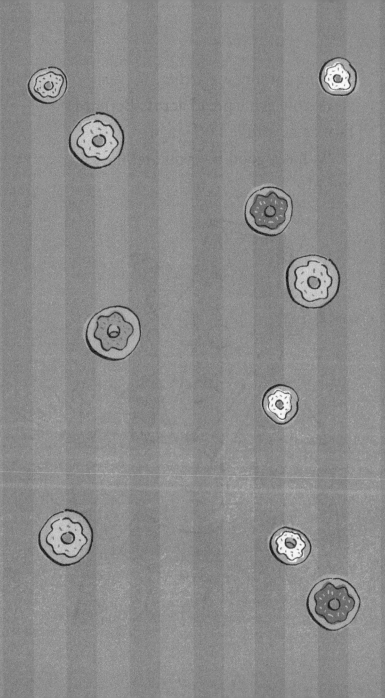

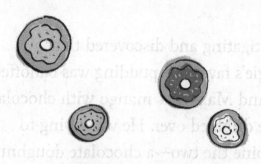

CHAPTER THREE

It was mid-morning the following day at the Amazing Bakery, and Sophie was serving in the shop because Amira had gone with Samuel to see the doctor. Freddie was in the kitchen experimenting with some doughnut recipes. Along with several other people, he was going to present Max and Margie with something special at the end of the show. He'd decided on doughnuts when he found out that they were their favourite treat. Freddie had also done some further investigating and discovered that Margie's favourite pudding was banoffee pie, and Max's was mango with chocolate sauce dribbled over. He was trying to combine the two—a chocolate doughnut with banana cream filling and caramel glaze for Margie, and a vanilla doughnut with mango filling and chocolate glaze for Max.

'Not enough chocolate in the dough, too much banana in the filling, and the mango's too sweet,' Freddie announced to Flapjack when he tasted his first attempts. Flapjack was snoozing in his basket, with one eye open in case Freddie dropped a doughnut by mistake.

Just then Amira walked into the kitchen with a heavy sigh, and Freddie could tell from her glum face that it was bad news.

'Poor Samuel has sprained his ankle so badly that he can't dance for at least six weeks, so that's us out of the show,' she said gloomily.

'Oh, Amira, I'm so sorry—that's really disappointing for you both.'

Amira nodded sadly and her eyes filled with tears.

Freddie paused. 'Have you thought about finding another partner? I'm sure Samuel wouldn't mind.'

'He suggested that too,' Amira said. 'And we thought of a couple of people from our dance class, but I've just spoken to them, and one is going on holiday and the other is too busy at work.' She sighed. 'Never mind, it just wasn't meant to be.' She tried to brighten up her face and force a smile. 'You shouldn't feel sorry for me. What about poor Samuel? Not only is he out of the competition, but he's also in pain!'

'I know,' Freddie replied. 'But it's still sad for you—it was your dream.'

'Oh well,' Amira said firmly. 'There's nothing to be done about it.' She pulled out her notebook, a pen, and a calculator and sat down at the table to do the bakery accounts.

Freddie began to make another batch of doughnuts, but his brain was whirring away. Amira was his best friend and he always wanted to try to help her, and perhaps this was the perfect opportunity for him to try to get over his stage fright.

'Would you like me to try?' he

asked her. Amira stared at Freddie in amazement.

'I don't think I could do the lift,' Freddie went on. 'But I learnt a little dancing at school, so I think I could manage the rest of it. Of course, I wouldn't be nearly as good as Samuel.' Amira didn't immediately say anything, so Freddie said, 'It's a terrible idea, isn't it? No . . . forget I ever said anything . . .'

'It's a **brilliant** idea!' Amira interrupted. 'I would love it! But what about your stage fright?'

'I'm going to overcome it,' Freddie replied decisively. 'Do you think you could teach me the steps? And can we take the lift out?'

'Of course! Most of dancing is just practice and because we work together we can fit in little bits throughout the day—

it will work beautifully. Oh Freddie, that's so kind of you!'

'It's my pleasure. Shall we start after work?'

'I think we'd better—we only have a week until the dress rehearsal,' Amira announced. Then she added cheerfully, in case Freddie was worrying, 'You can do an amazing amount in a week.'

'You can indeed,' Freddie replied, trying to ignore the twinge of nerves in his stomach.

An hour or so later, Freddie was about to go out on his deliveries when who should stroll into the shop but Bernard. He was clutching an **enormous** bunch of lilies and looking very dapper in a green tweed suit and a purple bow tie.

'Good afternoon, Freddie. Amira,'
he began. 'These are for you,' he said,
presenting the flowers to her.

'Thank you,' Amira replied, looking
slightly mystified.

'I was so sorry to hear the sad news
that Samuel won't be able to dance,'
Bernard explained.

'Yes, it is sad but—' Amira began.

'But never fear, Bernard is here!' Bernard interrupted, grinning. Before she could reply, he went on, 'I wanted to come and offer myself as a new partner for you. I know I am not trained yet in the steps, but I have always been well known for my grace and rhythm, so I am sure with a little practice I can be as good as Samuel. Probably better, in fact.'

Amira was so surprised that it took her a moment before she could reply. 'Bernard, that's so er . . . kind of you, but Freddie is going to take Samuel's place.'

Waves of jealousy cascaded over Bernard's face. 'But I thought that you were too scared to go on stage,' he hissed at Freddie furiously.

'I know, but I think it's the perfect time to try to get over that,' Freddie replied.

'You'll be fine,' Amira said cheerfully to Freddie. 'We'll practise loads. It'll be really fun.'

'I can be really fun too,' Bernard said desperately. 'And wouldn't you rather dance with me, a born dancer who doesn't get stage fright?'

Amira didn't want to hurt his feelings so she said, diplomatically, 'I'd hate to think I was distracting you from your magic, Bernard.'

'Oh, I'm not doing that any more,' he said quickly. Bernard always wanted to be taken seriously and had hated being laughed at by the Motions. 'I decided it was beneath me . . . ,' he said snootily before adding, '. . . so I will have oodles of time to devote to dancing.'

'I'm sorry, Bernard, but I've made my decision,' Amira said firmly.

'Very well,' Bernard said through clenched teeth, practically snarling at Freddie as he stomped out of the shop.

The following day, Bernard was still feeling cross about Amira dancing with Freddie rather than him, and so he decided to go to Tippy Top Tailors to cheer himself up by ordering a new suit. He had a custard-coloured tweed one in mind.

When he had nearly reached the shop, he noticed two familiar figures standing outside—Amira and Freddie. Flapjack was beside Freddie. *I wonder what they're up to?* Bernard thought, and he decided to spy on them to find out. He dived behind the parked cars along the pavement, and, using them for cover, crept along so he could hear what Amira and Freddie were saying.

'They do make such beautiful suits,' Freddie said. 'It's such a shame that they're so expensive.'

'Why don't you treat yourself? It might give you confidence,' Amira asked.

'No, I want to spend my savings paying for Sophie's patisserie course in Paris. And besides, I've got an old black jacket and trousers I can wear.'

Bernard rolled his eyes at this—why did Freddie always have to be so dull and kind?

'We should get going to the theatre if we want to have enough time to practise on stage before the Belville Ballet arrive for their rehearsals,' Amira said, and they walked off.

Bernard was torn between yellow tweed and spying on Freddie and Amira dancing. You're probably not surprised to hear that the latter won. Bernard followed Freddie and Amira along the streets and into the side entrance of the theatre. Once inside, Bernard scooted around to the auditorium so that he could watch them undetected. The auditorium was dark and empty, and he crept forward in the shadows to a point where he was near enough to hear what they were saying, but too far away to be seen.

The stage lights were on, and Bernard watched as Amira walked confidently out on to the empty stage. Freddie followed her, looking apprehensive, his eyes darting around the darkness.

'Don't worry, there's no one there,' Amira reassured him.

But Flapjack thought otherwise. Sensing Bernard, he began to bark at the darkness.

'Oh, do shut up, you annoying dog!'

Bernard cursed under his breath.

'Ssh, Flapjack,' Amira protested. 'You'll put Freddie off.'

Flapjack looked at her as if to say, *I'm only doing my job.*

'He's probably barking at a mouse,' she said to Freddie, as Flapjack sat down at the edge of the stage, keeping guard. 'Now, let's start with some basic steps.'

'OK,' Freddie said, still feeling uncomfortable. Amira began to show him, and he tried to copy her, but he was very stiff and stumbled a lot.

He's useless! Bernard thought with delight.

'I think music might help,' Amira said after a few minutes, and she went to put it on. She was right. The music relaxed Freddie, and his feet started to behave themselves. His face softened, and he

actually looked like he was having fun.
Suddenly, there was the patter of dainty
feet and a lot of excited chatter, as the
Belville Ballet Company burst into the
auditorium. The lights went on and
Freddie froze.

Cripes! thought Bernard, and he
ducked behind a row of seats and started
to crawl towards one of the exit doors.

'Hi, Freddie! Hi, Amira!' the ballet dancers called, as they all knew them from the bakery. 'What are you doing? Are you dancing? I didn't know you could dance! Show us some steps!'

The questions came thick and fast, and the dancers streamed down towards the stage. Poor Freddie felt like a rabbit caught in the headlights of a speeding car. All he could think about was getting off the stage. Amira, seeing how nervous he was, chatted away to the dancers, while gently herding him down the stage side steps into the auditorium and then out the door.

'I'm sorry that was such a disaster,' Freddie said, sounding downcast, as they walked back to the bakery. 'I just find the stage so big and empty when it's just the two of us.'

'It wasn't a disaster at all,' Amira said kindly. 'We just need to build your confidence and you'll be fine. Let's discuss it after work.'

'OK,' Freddie replied, trying to sound as cheerful as he could.

The afternoon came and went in a flurry of baking and deliveries, and before Freddie knew it, he was turning the shop sign to CLOSED and saying goodnight to Sophie as she left the shop for home.

'I've been thinking,' Amira said, as she finished tidying up the counter in the shop. 'Where do you feel most comfortable, Freddie?'

He thought for a moment. 'Either in my bed or in the kitchen.'

'That's what I thought you'd say,' she said. 'So since we can't practise in your bed, how about the kitchen? If we move the big table to one side, there is easily enough room.'

Freddie nodded. Dancing in the kitchen—that didn't seem scary at all.

'Yes, let's give it a go,' he said.

Meanwhile, in his flat above Macaroon's, Bernard was lying on his sofa, with Otto on his stomach, eating a bag of crisps and plotting. He had been to see the Motions earlier and told them he wouldn't be performing his magic act but that he would love to still be involved in the show—would it be possible for him to help backstage?

'*What d'ya think, Margie?*' Max had asked.

'Sure,' Margie had replied. 'We could always use more help backstage—just make sure that if you bring that cat of yours with you, you keep it under control.'

'Of course,' Bernard had simpered, delighted. The first part of his plan was in place.

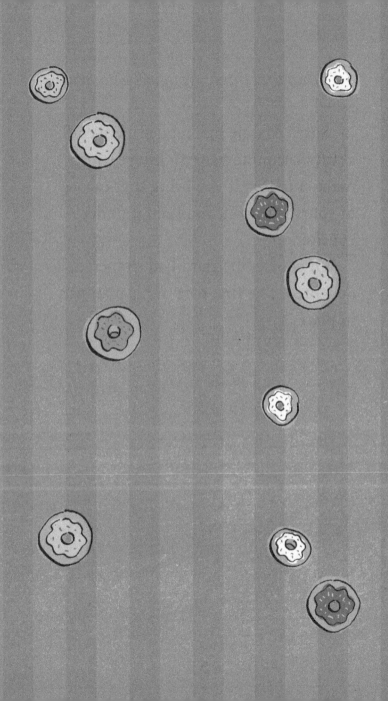

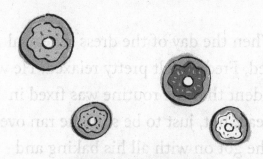

CHAPTER FOUR

Amira and Freddie spent the next week dancing around the kitchen whenever they could. They got up even earlier than normal, squeezed in little sessions during the day, and stayed up until midnight every night practising. They were both exhausted but happy because Freddie had really got the hang of the routine; Amira had simplified it a little and taken out the lift at the end. They also put together an outfit for him out of old clothes, and borrowed Samuel's hat and cane.

When the day of the dress rehearsal arrived, Freddie felt pretty relaxed. He was confident that the routine was fixed in his head, but, just to be sure, he ran over it as he got on with all his baking and deliveries.

But once he was at the theatre, it all became a bit too real—his anxiety began to build, and his doubts with it. What had he been thinking? He couldn't go out on that stage with Amira in front of lots of people and dance! He tried to distract himself by handing out some iced buns he'd made, but it was no good; he felt like he was trapped on a tiny boat headed for a giant waterfall. Before he knew it, the stagehands were ushering him and Amira up to the wings to wait while the act ahead of them finished.

'I really don't think I can do this,' he

said to Amira.

'Nonsense,' she replied firmly. 'You'll be fine.'

'No, I really won't be . . .' Freddie started to say, but then Bernard came over to them, grinning like a shark.

'Freddie, are you OK?' he asked with fake concern. 'You are looking terribly

nervous. Is there anything I can get you?
A glass of water?'

Freddie shook his head, thinking he
might be sick if he opened his mouth,
while Amira bristled with irritation—
the last thing she needed was Bernard
winding up Freddie.

'I'm surprised to see you here, Bernard,'
she said. 'I thought you weren't doing
your magic act.'

'I'm helping backstage—it's so
important to give back, don't you think?'
he said. When Amira didn't reply he went
on, 'Well, Freddie, whatever you do, don't
worry about the TV cameras and all the
thousands of people watching at home.'

'What TV cameras?' Freddie replied,
panicked.

'There aren't any,' Amira said in an
annoyed tone. 'He's just teasing you.'

'Yes, just my little joke, Freddie,' Bernard replied with a giggle. 'But seriously, would you like me to step in, Freddie? I brought my suit just in case; it wouldn't take me a moment to change . . .' he said hopefully.

Before Freddie could say anything, Amira replied, very definitely, 'No thank you, Bernard.' Just as Bernard was about to respond, the act on stage finished.

Amira took Freddie firmly by the hand and walked him on stage.

'Good luck!' Bernard called after them. Then he added gleefully in an undertone, 'You're certainly going to need it . . .'

Freddie wouldn't have thought it was possible to feel any more nervous than he already did, but when he saw the bright lights and Max Motion's blue eyes peering at him from the front row, he thought he might faint.

'Good luck, baker boy!' Margie said.
'I hope you dance as well as you bake.'

'Th . . . th . . . thank you!' Freddie stuttered.

His feet somehow arranged themselves into the starting position and, when the music began, he managed the first few steps. *Perhaps I will be OK*, he thought hopefully, and he could feel his confidence growing. But then something happened to the music—it sped up until it was going ridiculously fast. Freddie tried to keep up, but he stumbled and dropped his cane and hat.

'Don't worry. Just keep going,' Amira whispered.

But Freddie caught sight of Bernard roaring with laughter in the wings and could feel himself going to pieces again. He managed to shuffle through the rest of the routine until at last the music stopped.

'I'm so sorry,' Freddie said to Amira, feeling mortified.

'That was not your fault,' Amira said. 'Something went wrong with the music.'

'I know, but even without that I'm not sure I would have been OK. I find it so scary when it's just me and you on the stage with the bright lights shining on us—I feel so exposed.'

Meanwhile, Max Motion was saying, *'What d'ya think, Margie?'* to his wife.

'Well, you're just brilliant, honey,' she

said to Amira. 'But Freddie, you look like a frightened kitten with two left feet. I'm not sure dancing is for you.'

'No, I quite agree,' a voice said, and Bernard strode on to the stage, looking triumphant in his suit.

He was delighted; his tinkering with the music had worked perfectly. 'Mr and Mrs Motion, I am a very experienced dancer, and I really feel that I would be a better partner for Amira. Here, let me give you a little display.' Before they could say anything further he began to dance the beginning of their routine around the stage.

'What d'ya think, Margie?' Max said when Bernard had finished.

'Not bad,' Margie said. 'But it's not me who's dancing with him—what do you think, honey?' she said to Amira.

Amira replied immediately. 'Thank you, Bernard, for your kind offer, but I really think that Freddie and I can overcome his stage fright. He was brilliant in rehearsals, so I know he can do it. I think he just needs more practice performing in front of other people. So if it's OK with you, I'd like to stick with Freddie.'

Bernard looked furious, but he would never be rude to Amira, so he forced his face into a smile.

'*What d'ya think, Margie?*' Max said.

'I want to know what the baker thinks,' Margie said. 'Do you think you are up to it? Do you think you can change that much in a day?'

Freddie was really wavering, but Amira gave him such a pleading look and squeezed his hand so tightly as if to say, *Please, Freddie,* that he found himself saying, 'Yes, I think I can do it.'

'OK, honey, but I hope you're right because you're closing the show,' Margie said.

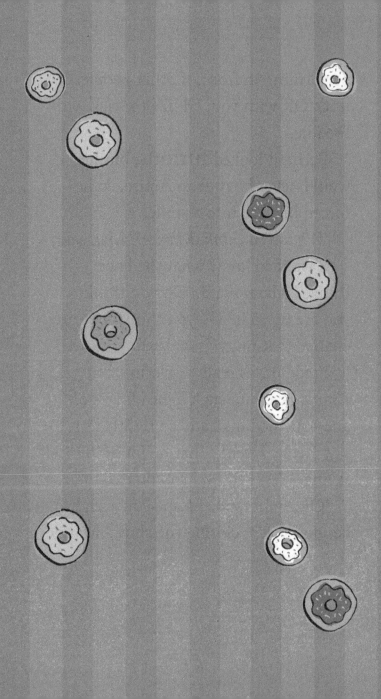

CHAPTER FIVE

But Freddie's confidence didn't last.

'I really think that was a massive mistake—you should definitely dance with Bernard,' Freddie said as soon as they were backstage. 'It's going to be a disaster, and I'm going to ruin the ending of Max and Margie's special show.'

'Nonsense,' Amira said firmly. 'There is no possibility of me dancing with Bernard. Don't worry, Freddie, I've got a plan. Now go home and get a good night's sleep, and I'll see you first thing in the morning.'

Freddie did as he was told. Flapjack was waiting for him back at the bakery, and they played together for a bit, but really Freddie was so tired that as soon as his head hit the pillow upstairs he was asleep. The next thing he knew, his alarm was going off and it was time to get up and get baking. Amira was already in the kitchen when Freddie arrived, sliding down the baker's chute with Flapjack on his knee.

'Shall we start dancing?' he asked.

'No, not yet,' Amira replied calmly. 'But we best get on with the baking as we've got a busy day ahead.'

'OK,' Freddie replied, and he decided to begin making the doughnuts for Margie and Max. As ever, the baking calmed his nerves perfectly, and he had soon almost forgotten about the show. Sophie arrived, and they baked peacefully together for an hour or so until it was nearly time to open the shop.

'Right, Freddie, let's show Sophie our routine,' Amira said. Freddie gulped nervously and was about to reply but Amira continued speaking. 'Sophie, would you mind joining in? Just to make it a bit less scary for Freddie.'

'I'd love that!' Sophie said excitedly.

'Will you show me the steps?'

'Of course,' Amira replied, beaming.
'I think you should just do a simple
step-together-step, a clap, and then
a glide.' Flapjack jumped out of his
basket and scampered around as Sophie
copied Amira. 'Yes, that's perfect,' Amira
pronounced when Sophie had done the
steps a few times. 'Right, let's get the
music on. Ready, Freddie?'

Freddie, who had taken off his apron
and picked up his hat and cane, nodded
apprehensively.

'Great, then let's begin!'

Freddie's first few steps were a little
jerky, but as soon as he saw that Sophie
wasn't really watching him but was
concentrating on her own dancing, he
began to relax, and the routine came as
easily as it had before.

'Bravo!' Sophie said when they'd
finished. 'You were great, Freddie!'

'Thanks, Sophie. It definitely made it
much easier having you dancing too.'

Amira looked at the clock. 'It's nearly opening time,' she said, and they took all the delicious cakes and pastries to the shop. Amira opened the front door. There were three people already waiting. They were regulars who Freddie knew well.

'Morning Colonel Cline, Mrs Frobisher, and Madame Bukowski, come in!' he greeted them.

'Hello everyone,' Amira said. 'I have a favour to ask you—would you mind helping Freddie and me with our dance routine for the Summer Talent Show tonight? It will take only five minutes.'

'Of course!' Mrs Frobisher said enthusiastically. 'What do you want us to do?'

'Well, if I showed you a few dance steps, do you think you could join in?'

'Absolutely,' she replied with a laugh.

'What a splendid idea!' Colonel Cline said. 'Nothing like a spot of dancing in the morning to set you up for the day.'

'What fun!' Madame Bukowski cried. 'But we'd better get going because I have to be at work soon.'

Amira showed them the same steps she'd shown Sophie, which they quickly grasped. More customers arrived and joined in.

'Right, let's begin,' Amira said and put on the music. Freddie, who had completely forgotten to be nervous, began. Before he knew it, he was into the routine and thinking about that rather than who was watching. Because the truth was, no one was really watching just him—even the customers who came into the shop were looking at everyone dancing.

When the routine finished, there was
loud applause.

'Again!' Mr Nightingale, who had just
come into the shop, cried.

'I must go, but take my place,'
Madame Bukowski said.

'Can we join in too?' asked Mr and
Mrs Patel, who had also just arrived.

Half an hour and a lot of dancing
later, everyone decided that they really
ought to get on with their days. But they
were all very excited to see Freddie and
Amira dance that night at the show.
'And if you dance like that, Freddie,
you'll bring the house down,' Colonel
Cline said.

'I'll try,' Freddie replied, still feeling anxious.

'Well, we'll all be in the audience wishing you all the best,' Mrs Patel said.

'Yes, and you know what they say, Freddie: dance like no one's watching,' the Colonel said.

Late morning was delivery time for Freddie, when he cycled around Belville with Flapjack, taking everyone's orders to them. He loaded all the boxes of cakes and other goodies on to his bicycle. Flapjack was in his basket and they were ready to set off when Amira came out of the shop.

'Hang on a moment, Freddie,' she said. 'I'm going to come with you.' She nipped round the back of the shop and returned a moment later with her bicycle that she rode to work.

'Can Sophie manage on her own?' Freddie asked.

'Absolutely,' Amira said. 'We'll only be a couple of hours.'

Their first stop was delivering a raspberry and white chocolate birthday cake to Mrs Chang in Water Lane. It was for her daughter, Ying. When Freddie and Amira arrived, a birthday party was in full swing.

'I hope you don't mind me asking . . .' Amira said to Mrs Chang after they gave her the cake, '. . .but Freddie and I are performing at the Summer Show tonight and we wondered if we could do our dance for the children?'

'I'm sure they'd love that,' Mrs Chang replied.

'Great! Do you think they'd like to join in too?' Amira asked.

'They'd love that even more!' Mrs Chang said with a laugh.

Amira and Freddie taught the children and Mrs Chang the steps, and then they all performed the dance together several times. In fact, the children were having so much fun that they didn't want Freddie and Amira to leave.

It was only when Mrs Chang brought in the birthday cake that Freddie and Amira could escape.

'See you tonight,' Mrs Chang said as she showed them out. 'And thank you so much!'

'Thank YOU!' Freddie said. 'That really helped me.'

Amira and Freddie cycled up Magnolia Canal and into the park to deliver the order for the café in the park.

'How are you feeling, Freddie?' Amira asked.

'Much better,' he said. 'But that's only because I've been dancing with other people. I'm worried that when it's just you and me on the stage tonight in front of an audience, I'll feel as nervous as ever.'

'Just take one thing at a time. At the

moment, we're building your confidence performing in front of other people,' Amira replied as they drew up outside the café.

Noah, a friend of theirs who ran the café, came out to meet them.

'Everything's ready,' he said with a wink to Amira.

Freddie looked puzzled.

'Great,' Amira said. 'Now, Freddie, follow me.'

By the side of the café was a large terrace with tables and chairs overlooking the lake. That day, because of the beautiful weather, it was crowded with people eating ice cream and drinking coffee, watching people swimming and boating on the lake. Noah had cleared a large area in the middle of the terrace, and Amira led Freddie over to it.

Freddie's stomach began to toss and turn, as Noah produced his megaphone and said, 'Hello everyone—I hope you are having fun. My great friends Freddie and Amira are dancing in the Summer Talent Show tonight.' Everyone cheered. 'But Freddie is feeling a little nervous, so would anyone like to come up here and dance with them to practise?'

Lots of shouts of 'Yes please!' followed.

'Excellent,' Noah went on. 'Amira will teach you a few steps, and then you can all dance together.'

It was another success with everyone joining in.

When it was finished, Amira turned to Freddie and said, 'Right, it's time now to do the routine on our own.' Freddie looked worried, but she went on. 'The secret is to just pretend everyone is there with you, and you'll be fine.'

Noah nodded, saying, 'And don't worry about what other people think—everyone makes mistakes when they do things—it really doesn't matter. No one will notice a few wrong steps as long as you look like you're having fun.'

Amira explained to the crowd what they were doing, and everyone sat down to watch. Freddie could feel his stomach beginning to somersault with nerves, but he tried to focus on all the advice he'd been given by Amira and Noah, and the Colonel earlier, and he told himself firmly, *I'm just going to enjoy this.*

And he did, for, although he made a few mistakes, he could see Noah was right—no one cared.

You might be wondering what had happened to Bernard. Well, he was still up to mischief. And it just so happened that he was sitting at one of the restaurants in Market Square, eating spaghetti Bolognese, when Freddie and Amira made their last delivery there.

It wasn't market day, but the square was crowded instead with tables and chairs spilling out from the restaurants. As it was lunchtime, every table was taken. Bernard watched as Amira and Freddie delivered some boxes of cakes to a restaurant and then stood, having a conversation. Amira was gesturing to an open space in front of a fountain in the middle of the square.

What on earth are they up to? Bernard wondered. Freddie looked very nervous, Bernard noticed with satisfaction. He didn't have to wait long to find out what was going on. Amira led Freddie to the space, set up a little portable speaker, and they began to dance. Almost immediately, everyone in the square stopped chatting and eating and looked over.

Freddie's pretty good, Bernard thought with irritation. *And even more annoyingly, he seems to have got*

over his stage fright. But then Bernard
gave a little chuckle. *Of course, that won't
last,* he thought. *After tonight, he'll never
be going near another stage in his life . . .*

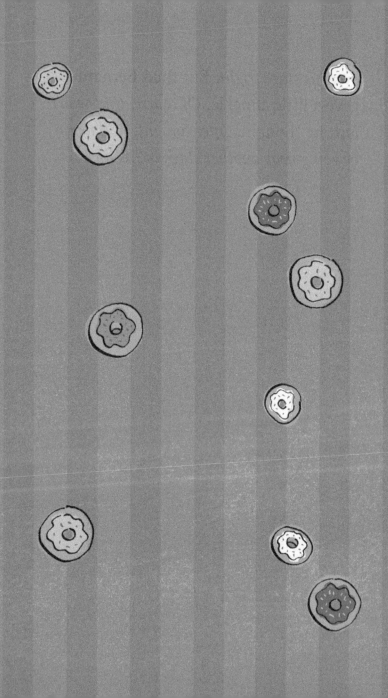

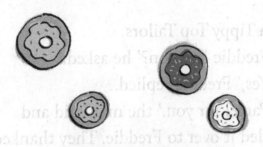

CHAPTER SIX

Freddie and Amira returned to the bakery, and Freddie spent the rest of the afternoon baking more doughnuts for everyone coming to the show. The show began at seven, so all the performers had to be at the theatre by a quarter past six. Freddie had decided to shut the bakery at five to give them plenty of time to get ready and over to the theatre. He was just turning the shop sign from OPEN to CLOSED when a delivery man drove up in his van and got out with a large parcel from Tippy Top Tailors.

'Freddie Bonbon?' he asked.

'Yes,' Freddie replied.

'Parcel for you.' the man said and handed it over to Freddie. They thanked each other, and the man drove off. Freddie carried the parcel into the shop and put it down on one of the tables.

'What's that?' Amira asked.

Freddie couldn't have been more surprised when he opened it, for inside was a beautiful black suit, a white shirt, a white waistcoat and tie, and a shiny new top hat and cane. There was a note saying:

GOOD LUCK!

It was signed 'From a friend.'

'It must be from Noah or Samuel,' Amira said.

'I guess so,' Freddie replied. 'That's so kind of them.' He tried on the suit, and it fitted perfectly. He put the hat on his head and twirled the cane.

'Well, at least I look the part now,' he said. Flapjack, who was sitting by him, gave a little growl. 'You are a strange dog sometimes,' Freddie said to him.

'What's not to like about this beautiful outfit?' Freddie said. Flapjack gave him a long-suffering look and went back to his basket.

Everything went smoothly backstage, and before Freddie knew it, a stagehand was walking up to them. 'Freddie and Amira, time for you to wait in the wings—you'll be on in a minute.'

Bernard was waiting for them there. He was unable to resist saying, 'My, my, Freddie, don't you look smart?'

'Thank you, Bernard—,' Freddie replied and was about to say that the suit, hat, and cane had arrived mysteriously in the post, but Bernard interrupted.

'—And how are you feeling?'

'I'm OK,' Freddie replied. The terrible sinking fear he'd had before had gone, leaving a nervy excitement in its place. But then he remembered how awful it had been when the music had gone wrong before. 'I'm pretty sure I'll be fine so long as nothing goes wrong,' he said.

'Don't worry about that,' Amira said confidently. 'I asked the stagehand to double-check the music—and what else can happen?'

'What indeed?' Bernard replied, his eyes twinkling.

The previous act—Mr Poots, the fire-eating optician—finished. They all clapped loudly as he came off stage, and Amira said, 'Right, Freddie, all set?'

'Absolutely!' Freddie replied, feeling the bubbles of excitement in his stomach.

'Remember to enjoy it,' Amira said as they walked hand in hand on to the stage and into the bright lights.

Freddie and Amira took their places. *Don't look at the audience,* Freddie told himself strictly, as he could feel his legs getting slightly wobbly.

'There may be trouble ahead . . .'

The song began to play, at the correct speed this time, and Freddie and Amira started to dance.

The first part of the routine was pretty easy for Freddie as he just had to do a few simple steps while Amira twirled around him. Then they both did a more complicated routine with a lot of fancy footwork. But Freddie managed it beautifully, and Amira caught his eye and gave him a big grin. *I really love this!* Freddie thought to himself, and he grinned right back at her.

The next section was a short solo of dancing by each of them while the other watched, making funny faces at the audience, pretending that they were competing with each other. Amira went first, and then Freddie began his section. But—oh dear—then something happened . . .

As part of his dance, Freddie came to the front of the stage and leant on his cane. But as soon as he put any weight on it, the cane collapsed, making him stumble and nearly topple into the audience.

What on earth? Freddie thought. He glanced over to the side of the stage and saw Bernard grinning with delight. Freddie realized with a jolt that it must have been Bernard who had sent him the suit and hat and booby-trapped cane, to sabotage his dance with Amira. 'I can't let him win,' Freddie told himself sternly, and he tried to follow Amira into the next section of the dance. But he was badly rattled and kept missing his steps.

Amira had also seen Bernard and realized what had happened. She gave Freddie a thumbs up and smiled encouragingly at him, and he did feel a little of his confidence seeping back. When he managed a tricky bit of the routine he thought, *Yes! This is going to be OK.*

But unfortunately Freddie was wrong, because Bernard's mischief didn't end there. As part of the routine, Amira and Freddie took off their hats and tapped them against their thighs, quite gently, but when he did so, Freddie's hat exploded with a loud **BANG** like a firework. The top of the hat flew off, and a **huge** puff of smoke came out.

Freddie, Amira, and pretty much everyone in the audience jumped a foot in the air and let out loud shrieks of surprise. Freddie threw the hat across the stage, and both he and Amira stopped dancing.

The audience started to laugh. Amira, playing along, grimaced and raised her hands in a comical way as if to say, *What can you do?* She turned to Freddie to check he was doing the same, but, to her horror, he was staring blankly at her like a zombie. His nerves had frozen him like a block of ice.

Oh no! Amira thought. *What on earth am I going to do?* She began to spin around Freddie, to look like it was part of the act, but she was thinking, *This is a disaster!* She looked desperately at the audience, hoping for a miracle.

And what she got was not quite a miracle, but it worked just as well.

It started with Sophie. Sophie felt so awful for Freddie and Amira that she had to do something, and the only thing she could think of was to join them. So she stood up and made her way up the steps at the side of the stage, with Flapjack scampering after her. She turned and smiled as she reached the top, beckoning people to join her. 'Come on up, if you know the steps!' she shouted.

Mr and Mrs Patel, Madame Bukowski, Colonel Cline, Mrs Chang, and the children and all the other people who had danced with Freddie during the day quickly got up too. Soon the stage was full of people dancing with Freddie and Amira.

The rest of the audience, thinking it
was all planned and part of the act, cheered
and clapped. At last, Freddie relaxed and

resumed his routine with Amira, who looked as if she might burst with relief.

'No, no, no!' Bernard cursed under his breath, stamping his foot in frustration. 'They're ruining my plan! And yet again, Freddie is going to come out looking like a hero. I can't stand it!'

He picked up Otto and stormed out

of the theatre, just as Amira whispered
to Freddie, 'Let's do the lift,' and before
he could protest, Amira put her hands
around Freddie's waist and lifted him
up above her head. The audience went
wild!

Three encores and a lot of
applause later, Freddie and Amira
stood at the front of the stage
along with all the other performers,
as Max and Margie came up on to
the stage.

'Well, that was one fabulous finale
to the show!' Margie said, and the
audience laughed. 'If you two weren't
so darned good at baking then I think
you could be dancing stars.'

'Thank you! Speaking of baking,
I have something for you,' Freddie
said. Sophie appeared from backstage
and handed him the box of special
doughnuts. He presented them to
Max and Margie. 'I know you love
doughnuts,' he said. 'I really hope you

enjoy these—I based them on your favourite puddings— a chocolate doughnut with banana cream filling and caramel glaze for you, Margie, and for you, Max, a vanilla doughnut with mango filling and chocolate glaze.'

'Oh my word! They look sensational! I just have to try one now,' Margie said.

'Me too,' Max agreed, and they took a doughnut each and bit into them.

The whole audience fell silent as they waited for the verdict, until someone shouted, *'What d'ya think, Margie?'* and everyone laughed.

'I tell you what I think,' she replied. 'That is heaven in a mouthful!'

Everyone laughed again.

'I agree. Pretty amazing!' Max said.

Other gifts were given to them—a beautiful bunch of flowers, a book of memories of the theatre that made Margie cry with delight, and even their portraits painted by a local artist.

'Oh, everyone, you have spoilt us so much!' Margie said. 'And you didn't need to because Max and I have loved every day of working here. But there is one last present that I would love from you all.'

'What's that, Margie?' someone shouted out from the audience.

'Well, I got the idea from Freddie and Amira's dance. You know it has always been my ambition to get all of Belville dancing, and we've got pretty much the whole of Belville here now, so that is what I'd like. Let's get the music back on and have everyone on their feet—let's dance! Oh, and Freddie and Amira, let's see that lift again!'

And so that is exactly what happened. The music boomed out and everyone leapt to their feet and happily danced the night away.

BORN to BAKE.
HAPPY to HELP.

Freddie Bonbon is the most AMAZING baker in town, so when the Belville Cake Competition is announced, everyone wants Freddie to win.

Everyone, that is, except rival baker Bernard, who will go to any lengths to make sure Freddie's showstopper cake is a raspberry-blowing DISASTER!

FREDDIE'S
AMAZING BAKERY

THE GREAT RASPBERRY MIX-UP

WRITTEN BY
**HARRIET
WHITEHORN**

ILLUSTRATED BY
**ALEX G
GRIFFITHS**

BORN to BAKE.
HAPPY to HELP.

Freddie Bonbon is the most AMAZING baker in town, but somebody loves his cakes so much they've stolen them! Who could have done such a thing?

And when superstar cat Cookie goes missing too, it looks as though the town has a mystery on its hands . . . could Freddie's little dog, Flapjack, be the one to solve it?

FREDDIE'S AMAZING BAKERY

THE COOKIE MYSTERY

WRITTEN BY
HARRIET WHITEHORN

ILLUSTRATED BY
ALEX G GRIFFITHS

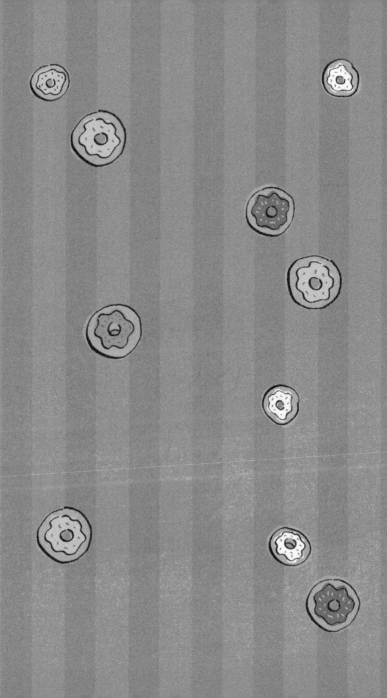

Harriet Whitehorn grew up in London,
where she still lives with her family. She is
the author of the Violet series (nominated
for several awards including the Waterstones
Children's Book Prize) and also the fantasy
duo, *The Company of Eight* and
The Conspiracy of Magic.

GLOSSARY

BAKE to bake food is to cook it in an oven, especially bread or cakes

BATTER a mixture of flour, eggs, and milk beaten together and used to make pancakes or to coat food before you fry it

BEAT to beat a cooking mixture is to stir it quickly so that it becomes thicker

BOIL to boil a liquid is to heat it until it starts to bubble

BRIOCHE a light sweet bread typically in the form of a small round roll

BUTTERCREAM a soft mixture of butter and icing sugar used as a filling or topping for a cake

CAKE sweet food made from a baked mixture of flour, eggs, fat, and sugar

CROISSANT a crescent-shaped roll made from rich pastry

DOUGH a thick mixture of flour and water used for making bread or pastry

ECLAIR a finger-shaped cake of pastry with a cream filling

FONDANT ICING a thick icing made from water and sugar

GATEAU a rich cream cake

GLACÉ ICING	a thin icing made with icing sugar and water
MARZIPAN	a soft sweet paste made from almonds and sugar
MELT	to melt something solid is to make it liquid by heating it
MERINGUE	a crisp cake made from the whites of eggs mixed with sugar and baked
MIX	to mix different things is to stir or shake them together to make one thing
MIXTURE	something made of different things mixed together
MOULD	to mould something is to make it have a particular shape
PASTRY	a dough made from flour, fat, and water rolled flat and baked
PROFITEROLE	a small ball of soft, sweet pastry filled with cream and covered with chocolate sauce
ROYAL ICING	hard white icing made from icing sugar and egg whites, typically used to decorate fruit cakes
SPONGE	a soft lightweight cake or pudding
STIR	to stir something liquid or soft is to move it round and round, especially with a spoon
TART	a tart is a pie containing fruit, jam, custard, or treacle
WHISK	to whisk eggs or cream is to beat them until they are thick or frothy

FREDDIE'S
DOUGHNUT MUFFINS

> YOU WILL NEED AN ASSISTANT, SO MAKE SURE THAT AN ADULT HELPS YOU!

These easy-to-make muffins are filled with sweet raspberry jam—yum!

INGREDIENTS

- § 200g plain flour
- § 1 tsp bicarbonate of soda
- § 250g golden caster sugar
- § 100ml natural yogurt
- § 2 eggs
- § 1 tsp vanilla extract
- § 150g melted butter
- § 4 tbsp raspberry jam

METHOD

1 Pre-heat the oven to 180°C (fan 160°C, gas mark 4). Lightly grease a 12-hole muffin tin.

2 In a large bowl, mix together the FLOUR, BICARBONATE OF SODA, and 150g of the GOLDEN CASTER SUGAR—this is your dry mix.

3 In a large jug or bowl, whisk the YOGURT, EGGS, and VANILLA EXTRACT together—this is your wet mix.

4 Pour your wet mix into the dry mix. Then add the MELTED BUTTER and stir everything together gently. Be careful not to stir the mixture too much.

5 Divide two-thirds of the mixture amongst the muffin tin holes, then add 1 tsp JAM to the centre of each. Top with the remaining mixture, making sure you can't see any of the jam.

6 Bake for 15–20 minutes until firm and golden. Leave the muffins to cool in the tin for 5 minutes, then lift out and coat in your remaining CASTER SUGAR.

7 Your sugary, jammy doughnuts are now ready. They are really delicious when eaten warm, so tuck in!

VOILA!

Here are some other great stories we think you'll love!